TUMBLE

For Finn, who challenged me to a story duel,
and for my Texas family, who showed me
the beauty of the southwest. —A.H.B.

Library of Congress Cataloging-in-Publication Data available

ISBN 978-1-338-82866-5

10 9 8 7 6 5 4 3 2 1   23 24 25 26 27

Printed in China 38
First edition, June 2023

Book design by Sarah Dvojack
Art direction by Brian LaRossa

The text type was set in KG Blank Space Sketch.

TUMBLE

Adriana Hernández Bergstrom

ORCHARD BOOKS • NEW YORK

Wind blows...

Tumble g o e s .

Fence stops.

Tumble hops.

Cactus waves.

Tumble stays

and stays . . .

and stays.

Rain

drops.

Tumble pops.

Thunder booms.

Tumble blooms.

Sun glows.

Tumble goes

and goes

and goes.

CAN YOU SPOT THE PLANTS AND ANIMALS?

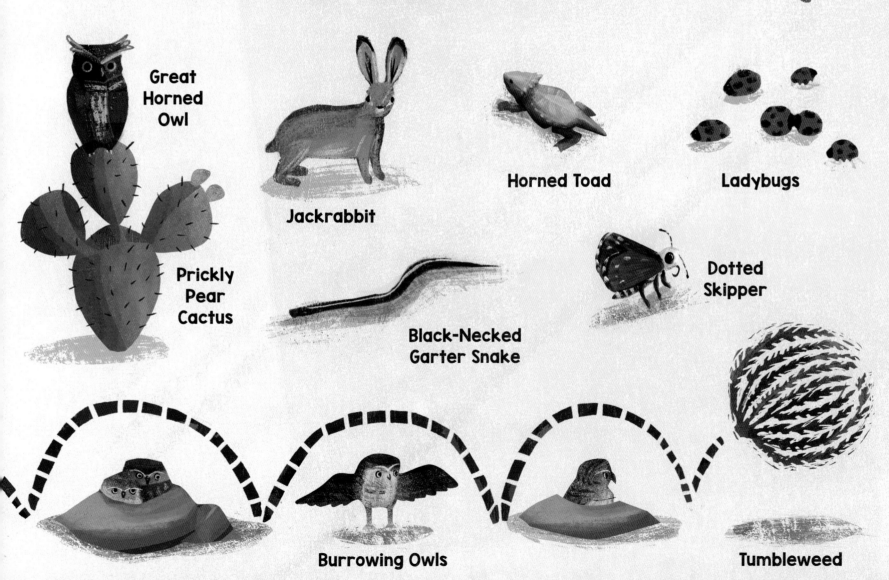

Great Horned Owl

Jackrabbit

Horned Toad

Ladybugs

Prickly Pear Cactus

Black-Necked Garter Snake

Dotted Skipper

Burrowing Owls

Tumbleweed

Gray Wolf

Hawk

Mesquite
Tree

Collared Lizard

Tarantula

Saguaro

Canyon Bats

Clouded
Sulphur

Baby Javelina

Roadrunner

FUN FACTS ABOUT TUMBLEWEEDS

Tumbleweeds are real plants. There are many different plants that are called tumbleweeds. All of them dry up and are moved by the wind. They spread their seeds by tumbling around wherever the wind takes them.

Most tumbleweeds are annuals. They seed, grow, flower, and dry up.

Tumbleweed flowers are SUPER small!

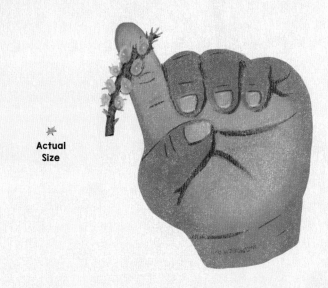

Actual
Size

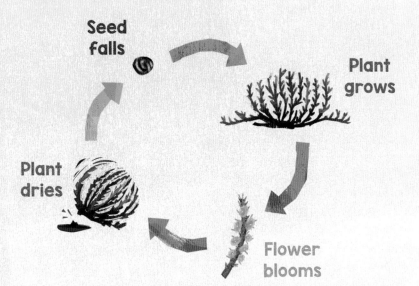

Seed
falls

Plant
grows

Plant
dries

Flower
blooms

Some tumbleweeds are pests. They grow so well that other plants can't find space to grow.

Tumbleweeds get stuck in lots of different places. They have even covered entire buildings and blocked roads!